Shipw

SUNNY COAST News

SHIP STRIKES REEF!
OIL SPILLS DISASTER!

A major emergency has occurred in our region overnight with the grounding of a large cargo ship on our local well-charted reef. The vessel is stuck fast on jagged rocks, creating a hazard to other shipping and local craft. Already vast quantities of highly-toxic oil are leaking into the sea, threatening the lives of thousands of marine creatures. Strong currents are carrying the oil onto beaches and bays all along our coastline, making survival difficult for fish, seabirds, crustaceans and shellfish.

written by Pam Holden
illustrated by Kelvin Hawley

1

One morning Charlie was shocked to read newspaper headlines naming the coastal town where he lived: SHIP STRIKES REEF! OIL SPILLS! Experts advised that the clean-up might take many weeks, announcing strict bans:

- *All beaches closed.*
- *Fishing and shellfish-gathering banned.*
- *No boating permitted.*

3

Charlie read that a shipwreck was a deadly threat to the sea creatures whose habitat was already becoming contaminated. He remembered his many visits to a small island close to the reef, to stay with his grandparents. He had watched the world's tiniest penguins, Little Blue Penguins (or fairy penguins), that lived there – swimming, fishing, and nesting on the rocky shores. Knowing they were in serious danger, Charlie hurried to the island, volunteering to join a rescue team. He could see the reef where the damaged ship lay stuck firmly, with poisonous oil leaking from its wrecked hull.

Charlie remembered which beaches had well-hidden nests in burrows or cracks between rocks, so he immediately led the searchers there. Several blackened, oiled birds were found, struggling as they were firmly removed from their nests by gloved hands, then gently placed into pet carrier crates. Charlie felt sorry for the Little Blue Penguins, because wild birds are totally unused to human contact, so this handling was extremely stressful for them.

How proud Charlie felt when he was chosen to help transport
these frightened birds to the Rescue Depot! Each bird was given
an identification number on an attached tag, then examined by
vets, weighed, and checked for injuries: all had thick oil clogging
their feathers; most suffered from stress and exhaustion; some
had broken wings or legs. A record was made of the date and
details such as the place they were found, so that after recovery
they could be returned to the same area.

Little
Blue
Penguin
Number
79

Charlie watched closely as penguins from his grandparents' island were put through these steps. He felt particularly worried about one little bird shivering with cold and exhaustion. Its legs and wings were not broken, but Number 79's feathers were thickly coated with sticky black oil. While other birds were treated for injuries, Charlie followed this special penguin through the steps in its recovery.

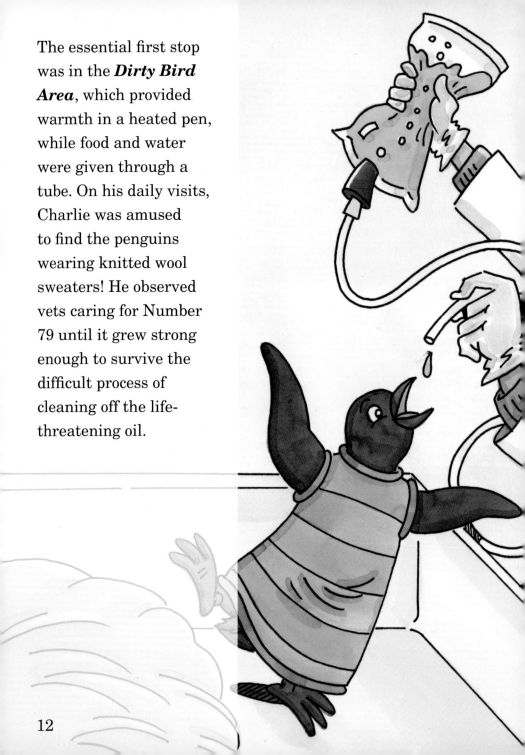

The essential first stop was in the **Dirty Bird Area**, which provided warmth in a heated pen, while food and water were given through a tube. On his daily visits, Charlie was amused to find the penguins wearing knitted wool sweaters! He observed vets caring for Number 79 until it grew strong enough to survive the difficult process of cleaning off the life-threatening oil.

In the **Washing Area**, getting rid of every speck of dark oil was a stressful experience for poor Number 79 – and for Charlie watching anxiously! Two experts worked together for almost an hour, using warm water, detergent, towels, and toothbrushes. This was followed by a thorough water rinse with a high-pressure hose – all causing wriggling and struggling!

15

As Number 79 was moved to the **_Clean Bird Area_** to dry under a warm lamp, Charlie noticed it looked more like a Little Blue Penguin usually does, with its white belly and dark blue feathers. It rested comfortably, snuggling close to other birds before settling into an exhausted sleep.

On his next visit, Charlie was relieved to see the little bird busy preening: using its beak to overlap its ruffled feathers back into place. Now 79 was clean, but not yet waterproof. That was something the penguins had to work on for themselves. Preening was vital to restore waterproofing by rebuilding natural oils in their feathers.

During the following days, Charlie saw encouraging changes: medicine was given to prevent infection; weight was checked; nourishing food helped to build strength. Twice daily, Number 79 had to be held wriggling by one person while being hand-fed by another with enormous amounts of anchovies and sprats eaten whole. Then swimming was allowed in a warm shallow pool with perching platforms for preening.

19

Finally Number 79 joined other recovering birds in an outdoor cold-water pool, gradually building strength – swimming, feeding, waddling, diving, preening – to prepare for release back into the wild. After many weeks, a final check showed that these Little Blue Penguins were healthy and fully waterproof, ready to be returned to their own environment.

Charlie took Number 79 in a pet carrier to the local beach, where an excited crowd gathered. All the children from his class assembled in a semi-circle, each with a plastic box containing a healthy penguin. "These are the lucky penguins that have survived the disaster," announced the Wildlife Expert. "We'll set them free to find their way home. Listen to Charlie's instructions."

"Penguins have strong homing instincts," shouted Charlie. "So get ready to open their boxes: 1, 2, 3, Free!" As the boxes were opened, the little penguins waddled out onto the beach, where most rushed straight into the ocean and began to swim through the waves.

A few penguins were confused about which direction was right, but they promptly received helpful guidance from the students – clapping, shooing and pointing! Soon all the little birds were swimming strongly toward deeper water, heading for their homes, back to freedom at last!